CW01629448

Titles in the *Choose Cthulhu* Series:

1. **THE CALL OF CTHULHU**
   Leandro Pinto
2. **AT THE MOUNTAINS OF MADNESS**
   Edward T. Riker
3. **THE SHADOW OVER INNSMOUTH**
   Giny Valrís
4. **THE NAMELESS CITY**
   Giny Valrís
5. **THE DUNWICH HORROR**
   Leandro Pinto
6. **THE DREAMS IN THE WITCH HOUSE**
   Edward T. Riker
7. **THE ARKHAM MADHOUSE**
   Leandro Pinto, Giny Valrís, and Edward T. Riker
8. **THE COLOR OUT OF SPACE**
   Edward T. Riker
9. **THE FESTIVAL**
   Jen D. Pine
10. **THE WHISPERER IN DARKNESS**
   Giny Valrís
11. **THE HAUNTER OF THE DARK**
   Leandro Pinto
12. **THE THING ON THE DOORSTEP**
   Leandro Pinto
13. **THE SHADOW OUT OF TIME**
   Giny Valrís
14. **THE CASE OF CHARLES DEXTER WARD**
   Edward T. Riker

CHOOSE CTHULHU BOOK 4

The Nameless City

Giny Valrís

Illustrations: Eliezer Mayor

TRANSLATED FROM THE SPANISH BY
CARLA LÓPEZ MEDEROS

Page layout by Patricia H. Albín
English edition by Carla López Mederos
Copy translation by Jonathan Green
and Lee Braddock

At Steve Jackson Games

President/Editor-in-Chief: Steve Jackson
Chief Executive Officer: Philip Reed
Chief Operating Officer: Susan Bueno
Chief Creative Officer: Sam Mitschke
Production Manager: Sabrina Gonzalez
Production Artist: Alex Fernandez
Prepress Checker: Susan Bueno
Project Manager: Darryll Silva
Operations Manager: Randy Scheunemann
Director of Licensing: Alain H. Dawson
Director of Sales: Ross Jepson

Choose Cthulhu, the pyramid logo, and the names of all products published by Steve Jackson Games Incorporated are trademarks or registered trademarks of Steve Jackson Games Incorporated, or used under license.
Choose Cthulhu Book 4 – The Nameless City
is copyright © 2023 by Steve Jackson Games Incorporated.

Choose Cthulhu is a trademark of Edward T. Riker and is used under license.
Choose Cthulhu characters are copyright © 2020 by Edward T. Riker.
All rights reserved.

The scanning, uploading, and distribution of this material via the Internet or via any other means without the permission of the publisher is illegal, and punishable by law. Please purchase only authorized electronic editions, and do not participate in or encourage the electronic piracy of copyrighted materials. Your support of the author's rights is appreciated.

WARNING!

How many times have you felt like screaming "Don't do that, you fool!" when reading a book or watching a movie?

Well, this is your chance to be the one to make the decisions! You'll find many different actions to carry out within the pages of this book.

As you read through the story, you'll choose what you want to do. Your decisions will determine whether you successfully complete your investigation, die a horrible death, or spend your last days in a mental institution.

Only you are accountable for your destiny. It is up to you to save (or condemn) the world. It's very simple: once you've read what's happening, follow the instructions to find out where your choices take you. Take into consideration that you can't go back; read your options carefully and think before you choose. In the ***Choose Cthulhu*** books, you'll not only enter the world crafted by H. P. Lovecraft, but you'll also have the chance to relive his dark creations. Do you think you can outsmart the children of the master himself?

Oh, and when in doubt: "Ph'nglui mglw'nafh Cthulhu R'lyeh wgah'nagl fhtagn."

1

Your name is George Aberdeen. Miskatonic University has sent you on an archaeological expedition to the desert of Araby. You have now been lost for several weeks. Your wineskin is almost dry and the scorching sun, which never takes a day off, comes out beyond the burnt horizon.

You struggle to remember how it all started. How is it possible that only a month ago you were at peace in your house near the campus, skimming a book? And how is it that what you found in that ancient copy – a manuscript that you had borrowed from the Miskatonic Library of Incunabula to write a report – has led you to one of the most inhospitable areas on the face of the Earth in search of an illusion? A nameless city . . .

Your chapped lips hurt when you laugh. You laugh because it's hard to accept that your life has taken such a drastic turn and that, from the comfort of your Victorian house, you've ended up balanced on top of this stinking animal, blinded by the mirages of the sun and about to collapse?

You remember that book very well – it was Gaspard du Nord's translation of the volume entitled "Livre d'Ivon." And you remember what you came across in that book just by chance: Its back cover, which had been worn by age, revealed a hidden parchment. You removed it with extreme care, thinking you had found a philological treasure. The parchment you found was yellowed, age-worn, and written in Arabic . . .

Turn to page 3

Of *course* you remember that book. And you remember what you found hidden in the back cover, just by accident, which led you on this wild adventure . . .

3

Excited, you asked your family's old attorney, Albert A. Baker, for help. Not only did he study law, but in his youth, he studied the languages of the Arabic countries, including some rare dialects. He was the one who helped you translate that manuscript, and he was the first to be frightened by the horrific potential of what it contained.

When did you decide to willingly give in to madness and unreason? Was it at the very beginning, when the words "desert of Araby" or "apocryphal nightmares of Damascius" came out of the translation? Or was it near the end, when the shaking hand that penned that snaky writing put a name for the first and last time to The Nameless City?

The Nameless City! Such an enticing spell enveloped you upon reading those words! A curse of Araby and places no civilized man had ever set foot in!

That ancient parchment became an obsession. In the following days, you sought advice from some of your colleagues, such as Henry Armitage, whose doctorate in Letters and Philosophy qualified him as one of the best-trained minds in the university. You were excited to show him your finding, and he, just as excited, helped you figure out the most obscure excerpts and their connection to Damascius, the eclectic Greek philosopher.

Intrigued, turn to page 40

4

You scream and howl at the wind, raising your arms like a religious fanatic. If it really is the spirit of the desert, it'll welcome you, and it might find a reason in your devotion and spare your life.

Then, something unprecedented happens: the winds literally sweep you off your feet. You hover in the air as if held by a translucent hand. And the face made of sand twists and shifts, but it remains there. There's no doubt of its existence – it's definitely there! That's the face of an undiscovered power that controls the storm!

Dragged by it, your unsettled eyes see a sea of sand roll underneath you at full speed, as if you were on a plane. Little by little, you pick up enough speed to make the touch of the air become igneous, reducing your limbs to burnt-out stumps. Seas, continents, and oceans sweep beneath you, and you see it all with your insane eyes. It's as if you were looking at yourself from the outside, beyond pain, beyond comprehension . . . seeing yourself as a trophy the gods had selected.

Whatever that thing is, it has chosen you as its prey. And it's dragging you north – to the edge of the world – where it must live . . . and where it takes its prey. You hear a last cry in the wind in which you fancy you distinguish a word . . .

Turn to page 5

5

I . . . THA . . . QUA . . . the wind whispers, the tempest yells, the skies and galaxies scream. I . . . THA . . . QUA . . . some tiny figures shout down there, somewhere that is not sand anymore, but covered in white snow. They are cultists, followers that sing to the sky, where the northern lights have taken a slightly human shape (that of their original god) and examine them from above with stars for eyes. The eyes are worshiping them, and you too, for you are hanging from up high, like a piece of meat that the friction of inhumane, meteoric, comet-like velocities has half-burned . . .

You also start screaming, "Ithaqua, Ithaqua!" knowing full well that you are the prey chosen for the sacrifice. You've become food for gods.

THE END

6

Rightly so. Although some symbols appear upside down and others are extrapolations, no one here has inquired not about the type of symbol, but their number. And if there are four stone pillars, that means there are only four symbols. Well thought!

You decipher a mathematical key with which to interpret the meaning of these hieroglyphs. You conclude it is a solar calendar; it's got nothing to do with our sun, but with a faraway star in the Puppis constellation that is only visible at certain moments of the year. Word has it that it's one of the hottest stars in the universe: a small, white dwarf only three times the size of the earth. Seemingly, the obelisks count down the unfathomable time left for it to cool down and become a black dwarf. What horrible astronomical meaning will that occurrence have when it takes place in . . . uh, let me see . . . 5 × 4, plus the cosine of the square root of pi (you do the math mentally) . . . a trillion years, give or take a century?

The hieroglyphs don't say so, but it's bound to be related to the awakening of "Something" that now lies asleep among the clouds of space dust, somewhere where there's only coldness and darkness . . .

Return with a shiver to the general map on pp. 102-103 and keep exploring

7

Obviously, before Everest was discovered, it was still the world's highest mountain, only no one knew it. So, the answer must be the word "Everest."

You push the springs and levers that correspond to those sounds, and the door to the temple opens. You step into a bleak darkness, so dense it seems to be furry and its little hairs slide across your face, tickling you. It's a very unsettling feeling, as if darkness were liquid and you could push it away with your arm or swing it in languid tides.

You light your alcohol burner and discover a staircase that descends in darkness to the floor below. There's no doubt it's under the level of the sand outside.

It sounds unsettling, but since you're here now, what could you do but explore everything?

Raise your burner and explore the unknown on page 20

8

You think it best to stay away. Stories about bloodthirsty tribes of the desert reached your ears before you left Riyadh. They are most protective of their patch of sand, and they could behead any foreigner who dared set foot on it.

You guide your animal in the opposite direction – you can't tell if it's the way you came from or if you're taking a different path. (You don't even care; right now, the desert looks all the same to you, dry and blazing.) You're in luck: Apparently the men didn't see you because they don't walk toward you or shoot their rifles.

However, your excitement is short-lived. Soon you realize you are completely on your own. You squeeze the wineskin, but not even the tiniest drop of water will come. There's nothing left.

The sun overhead is its own galaxy of ardent and cruel light. Heat rises from the stones in the path.

Turn, parched, to page 9

9

Your camel suddenly comes to a halt. You don't understand why. You whip him with the bridle to make him move, but after staggering for a couple of seconds, he collapses onto the sand. You roll as if you'd fallen from a tree. When you stand up, you see he doesn't move. He's dead.

Without a second thought, you draw your knife and stab the humps. You look for the last drop of liquid he stored before it evaporates. The air shimmers and forms inverted waterfalls, shaking the desert's heat on the horizon.

To your right, the east – according to the movement of the solar star – a brown wall rises, which could be the prelude to a sandstorm. To your left, the terrain descends slightly until it meets faraway flashes. Something metallic that shines, perhaps? More bandits? What will you do? You can't stay here beside your dead camel.

You'd better start walking, or you'll be the next to become a rock in the desert.

If you head toward the storm, turn to page 46
If you walk toward the flashes that you see in the distance, go to 14

10

Four pillars that look like cracked obelisks emerge from the ground. They seem to sprout around a common nucleus, like fingers of a buried hand. You step closer and see there are scratches on the stone near the top of the pillars. You hug the first obelisk and start climbing. You find it hard at first and you fall a couple of times (thankfully the sand is soft). But you are determined and manage to reach the top.

Undoubtedly, these are a sort of hieroglyph, but they look nothing like the Egyptians' or Chaldeans', nor do they resemble those of any ancient civilization. The antiquity of these scratches reminds you of Sarnath the Doomed, and of other cities of the forgotten land of Mnar. They don't represent any living creatures, not even humanoids, but they seem like a complex clutter of ideograms with some numeric correlation.

You spend more than an hour climbing up stone fingers like a monkey, reading inscriptions until you eventually convince yourself that there really is a mathematical connection hidden somewhere. The problem is, it's so cryptic that you don't know what it is. But a privileged university mind like yours shouldn't have a hard time figuring it out.

Throwing your hands up in despair, turn to page 11

11

Suddenly, a ray of sun rests on the top of the obelisks and is refracted in many light beams. It's a beautiful scene because the light seems to needle its way through, like a mesh of fine threads of light that ties the stone pillars together.

There's an equivalence in the connected symbols – there's an icon at the top of each pillar and, in front of each of these, another three are mirrored. Two are upside-down, and another two look like a mathematical extrapolation of the first. How many symbols are there in total?

If you know the answer, add 2 to the result and go to the corresponding page. (If that page does not make sense, you'd better check your math!) Otherwise, return to the general map on pages 102-103 and keep exploring

12

You pull the combination of levers that results in that number, but something bad happens. The floor crumbles at your feet!

You fall with a huge cascade of dust until solid ground breaks your fall. The waves of pain confirm that you have a broken leg. You yell for help, but no one is listening.

You find yourself in an underground gallery where the temperature is several degrees lower than the outside. Many degrees. Your teeth start chattering and your breath becomes white, puffy clouds in front of your face.

The hours go by and the terrible truth starts to sink in. You are trapped and no one will come for you, no matter how much you scream. Soon, the internal bleeding will overcome you in a painful and debilitating way. Then the wind blows, and a powerful gush of air pushes you inside the gallery, rolling you along in a heap.

Turn to page 13

13

You roll and roll in waves of pain until you reach a subterranean lake. Your body is half-submerged, but even though your feet don't reach the bottom, you don't drown due to the high level of salinity in the water.

Your burner has broken, so you wait in the darkest gloom for something, anything, to happen as you fight the agonizing stabs of pain that run along your calf. But nothing happens. Not that day, not the next, not the following . . .

You end up petrified, another statue added to the collection of the geological cycle of the depths of the desert. Maybe, one day, an archaeological expedition will find you and rack their brains to try and reconstruct your story.

THE END

14

These flashes point to civilization. Or maybe they are reflective schists. More rocks and sand. But there's something strange about them; they blink as if their source were a moving mirror. Rocks don't do that. So you head in their direction, for the alternative would be to remain where you are. And that, obviously, would bring you death.

You walk a few miles with your gaze fixed on that blinking blaze. Feverish images cross your mind – crystal creatures that wander the desert, sand djinn like the ones that inhabit the legends of Araby. But you are not scared; your desperation to find someone or something to help you survive is bigger than the harm that may exist in old folk tales.

Suddenly, a flash of blue fills the horizon. You start to worry about your sanity. Are you dreaming – or are you seeing water?

Water! It's water! It was a moving river that created those flashes! With barely any strength left, you break into a run, consuming your remaining energy. If it turns out to be a mirage . . . you're dead.

Turn, hopeful, to page 15

15

A river! You're saved! But in Araby, near the Rub Al-Jali desert, there are no permanent water streams or lakes. This must be one of those rivers that come and go depending on the time of the year.

Red boats sail purposefully downstream; you see skiffs entangled in papyrus sedges. You wave at them, desperate, until the sailors spot you and come pick you up. Their language and their manner of dress confirm they are from around here, experts in shipbuilding and joinery.

They are good and kind people, even to foreigners who naively step into the Al-Jali without a native guide. They return you to civilization, to Salalah, where you spend many months recovering before you try your luck with your adventure again.

Return to page 1 and, this time, be more careful.
The desert may betray you.

16

Obviously, if by the 17th hour it's full to the brim, and each hour it's filled twice as much as the previous hour, the answer is that it'll be half-full an hour before the time is up. So you wait until that time of the day, crossing your fingers that you are not wrong, and you jump toward the darkness at the bottom of the well.

You fall and fall down an endless, pliable darkness . . . until your feet meet the bottom. You roll in the midst of a sand explosion, but you've been lucky – you haven't broken anything! It's cold down here, a glacial coldness that makes your bones creak. It's such an abysmal change in temperature that it seems as though the sun has not touched these parts in ages.

You find holes and odd niches in the walls. A weak musical note echoes in those cubicles as the main passageway is filled with sand. It must be the secondary tunnels that keep that peal going when it's drowned in the main one.

A swirl in the sand becomes the old god's fingers, playing a tune in that stone organ. It must be a millennium-old tune, immune to the touch of time. The other niches chant along with vibrations in an odd psycho-musical organ. This is a sound for demented ears, played in an auditorium from the beginning of time.

Examining these niches, you find a number of altars that appear to be designed for long-forgotten rituals of inexplicable origin; you are not sure to which primitive cult they belong. In one of them, you find something incredible.

Turn to page 17

17

You find that one of the niches is filled with what seems to be some sort of metallic machinery. Machines! Tubes and gears and iron arms that don't seem to follow the logic of steam technology or any other known to man.

After you've spent a considerable amount of time studying them, and before the sand buries them completely, you find a switch on a corner. It's shaped like a disc and full of etchings where some sort of disc-shaped key could fit.

Is that what it takes to get this extraordinary mechanism going?
If somewhere along this adventure you've been given a medallion that represents a reptilian creature, turn to page 27
Otherwise, leave this hole before you are buried in sand, return to the main city map on pages 102-103, and choose another destination

18

Since you have nothing better at hand, you grab one of the femurs of the many corpses that are piled at your feet. You hear the kneecap snap free – the bone is cold and porous. It's really disgusting.

Sadly, it's of no use against the thing that won't stop repeating the words "Abhoth, Abhoth!" as if they were a psalmody. A stream of acid shoots from its deformed mouth, melting the bone you intended to use as a weapon along with your right hand, which becomes a gross, gooey mass. The remaining parts of your fingers resemble macaroni. You scream in pain. It's as if you'd put your whole hand in a bucket of sulfuric acid.

You fear the anti-graverobbers trap has indeed done its job since, without a doubt, this is . . .

THE END

19

You resolve to go through the door, but you find a mechanism that blocks it. It looks like an ancient gearbox that seems to be based on a verbal riddle that will activate some of the levers. The riddle is the following: "Before Everest was found, what was the highest mountain in the world?"

Count the number of letters in the name of the mountain you seek, and go to the resulting page to open the door

20

You climb down the gloomy staircase. Your burner is an oasis of golden light in a swamp of shadows. Dark upon dark, night upon night. Dark rags against an obsidian cloth. And still, the light makes its way like an oil stain flowing on the greasy belly of the clouds.

When you reach the bottom, you find a spacious, low-ceilinged hall that is profusely decorated. A large statue of a two-faced god stares at an odd device. The contrast between those two faces overwhelms you – the main one is the color of marble, its expression serene, priestly. The other is turned to the wall – a horrible face, like a skinless human whose map of muscles frames a mouth with sharp teeth and eyes that sparkle madly. It's a twisted countenance filled with an insane and cannibalistic hunger.

Two sides of the same thing: Good and Evil.

Carefully muffling your steps, you walk up to the display, for it seems to hold a very old object.

Turn to page 21

21

You can't believe your eyes. What you are seeing might just as well come from a cinematograph (which has left many with their jaws hanging at your country's fairs). This device doesn't resemble anything built in the 20th century. It rather seems brought from the future, or from some dreamworld dimension. It resembles a rifle or some sort of grotesque gun, but it's bulky and full of valves and tubes that remind you of a steam engine. Swollen and twisted, many funnels protrude from its sides, and crystal cylinders sprout like lumps around both the top and the bottom.

When you hold it, you notice it is heavier than any man-made gun. But is it really a gun? Or is it a technological invention taken straight out of H. G. Wells' fantasies?

You notice a button on one side.

If you aim at the wall and push the button, turn to page 104
If you'd rather keep the object and try to leave the temple, go to 95

22

You venture farther into the brooding ruins, hidden under the sand like an ogre under a coverlet, and you make it to one of the buildings whose outline stands out. It looks like a dilapidated temple. It's very old, and the decorations on the walls resemble the friezes from Lower Egypt. But in this case, they are arranged following a hexagonal pattern, as though . . . yes, as though the walls were covered in snake scales.

The very entrance to the building reminds you of a giant snake's mouth whose fangs the architect turned into columns, and in the deep sockets of its eyes lie shiny lapis lazuli stones.

The unnatural, mechanical sound of strangely familiar music emerges from this place, swept by a strong gale that manifests from the serpent's mouth. The immense snake's throat must be connected either to the large galleries or to exits to distant places of the desert.

You pluck up the courage to light your burner – and step into darkness.

Turn to page 23

You are surrounded by a gloom so heavy that even the light of your burner struggles to find its way. But one thing is clear: This was once a great city, very powerful, such as Ur or Babylon were in their time. And you wonder about the origins of such greatness.

The temple is lower on the inside. The magnificence of its walls becomes a labyrinth of low ceilings and claustrophobic chambers that make no sense at all. You see many complex scratches on the wall that could be read as hieroglyphs. They show images of a very industrious city of great technological and social prowess.

But what really gets your attention, apart from the fact that these coarse figures resemble reptiles rather than humans, is that no picture represents death. It's a curious omission, since most primitive cities were more than obsessed with the concept and the rites of passage to the other life. These beings, however, don't worship or represent death in their friezes. It's as if for them, extinction – both at a personal and collective level – were an extravagant idea, and they somehow aspired to find eternal life.

Turn to page 24

24

You walk to a collapsed wall that won't let you through. However, in an adjacent corridor, you find a game of levers and symbols that might well be numbers. It looks like a mathematical progression etched on stone, incomplete. It's the following:

$$12345 \approx 0$$
$$90812 \approx 4$$
$$45501 \approx 1$$
$$88303 \approx 5$$
$$09086 \approx ?$$

What number will follow and replace the question mark, and what will happen when you complete the series?

If you pull the lever for 1, turn to page 12
If you pull the one for 3, turn to 81
If you pull the one for 6, turn to 71
If you pull the one for 9, turn to 45

You hope that the oily gas that will spill if you break the burner will set it alight and harm the creature. Praying it'll work, you hurl it so that it cracks upon impact, and it does! The burner is resistant, for it is designed for explorers, but the forcefulness with which you smash it against the creatures "head," if that's what you want to call it, cracks it. Moments later, it combusts.

The monster's screams of pain are impossible to describe. The slimy monstrosity convulses, rolls over the pile of bones (reducing them to dust) . . . and, although it is not dead, it withdraws, engulfed in flames, to the bottom of the hole.

Without a second thought, as soon as it has gone through the hole in the wall, you thrust your boot in there. You use it as a step to climb out of the well, although you know the Thing is right there, a few inches from your foot. But the pain is keeping it too busy to pay you any attention, and it doesn't attack.

You climb safe and sound to page 26

26

You can't believe your luck. But remember, you won't have your burner for future expeditions around the city.

Now, return to page 24 and choose another lever
Or return to the main map on pages 102-103 and pick another destination

The medallion that al-Fayid gave you in his tent pops into your mind, and you see it has the exact diameter to fit there. The imprints on the machine seem to be an exact mirrored replica of the ones on the medallion! Could it really be some sort of key?

With a racing heart, you insert it and press. Nothing happens. You turn it clockwise. Still, nothing happens. But then you turn it counter-clockwise . . . and the machine is set in motion!

There are some clicking noises, and from the heart of the gearbox come electric arcs. There's a spinning sound and suddenly an explosion of light drowns you. The energy courses through your body and drenches your skin, dripping into your muscles and boiling your blood, modifying your bones as if they were clay . . .

You feel trapped in a vortex of electric light and kinetic movement. You spin and spin uncontrollably inside a whirlpool of light, a pit whose walls are made out of arcane, supernatural energy. And you scream, because the terror is too intense even for your scientific mind. When you stop spinning, everything is changed. And not just your surroundings. You, too.

Turn to page 29

Suddenly, a burst of energy comes from the odd artifact.

29

Reality returns in a distorted way, adding color upon color as if a ray of sun penetrated a well of shadows, dark as a witch's cauldron. The colors are not right; the proportions slip down your retinas as if they had the shape of a spindle. Even gravity is not right. Or is it your center of balance that has been displaced?

You are not in the well anymore. Your surroundings have changed: You find yourself in a very different place – a sort of temple seen from the inside, where the walls are made of batholiths of carved stone. It's night, not day, but the moon casts an odd light. From that same moon, visible through a skylight, it appears that strands are hanging down.

All around you, there are . . . things. Beings of an extraneous and chaotic morphology; masses of lizard-like flesh, shielded behind armors of scales bigger and more massive than any human. They stare and shout at you. They prod you but they won't attack. Why?

You realize the horrible truth when you examine yourself: There are only three fingers on each of your hands, including an opposable thumb, and your skin has turned to scales. Your own body is as massive as these two-legged reptiles that surround you, and your eyes split symmetrically on either side of the same long snout scalloped with teeth.

You've become one of those things, one of those two-legged dragons!

And you hold a knife with your right hand . . . or should I say – your right claw?

Turn to page 30

30

"What sort of nightmare is this?" you wonder, as the other beings lead you, kindly but insistently, to the outside of the temple. Only in a terrible drug-induced state of derangement and delirium could a soul descend to hell like yours just did.

Outside the temple, you see an altar on which a human has been tied. It's a ritual sacrifice! And you have the sacred knife in your reptilian hand. Your sanity finally snaps when you look at the horizon surrounding the pyramid on whose cusp you are standing. It's not a barren desert, but a prehistoric forest that is dense and phantasmagorical, full of unnameable creatures. A forest that covered this part of the world long before unspeakable cataclysms led to a change in the climate in the dark times. In the distance, far away, you can make out a shore. The shore of the sea that led to the center of Araby before the Last Stone Age.

The human, with a primitive cranium structure like a Cro-Magnon, stares at you with wild, fear-shot eyes. He begs for his life in a language that hasn't been heard on earth for millions of years. Thousands of other prehistoric beings kneel by the base of the ziggurat, worshiping their gods while the draconian creatures keep them at bay with objects of exotic technology.

Slowly, acting the part of high priest, you raise your sacrificial dagger . . .

What will you do?

If you sacrifice the poor human, turn to page 66
If you refuse and try to free him from the altar, turn to 44

Judging by the remains of his clothes, it's clear this is a survivor of a previous expedition. And then it hits you! His skewed chin, curious eyes, and the scars of long-ago smallpox all over his face finally fall into place: It's your colleague from the Research Society at Miskatonic, Sir Richard Burton! You remember that a year ago he left for the desert of Araby (although, supposedly, somewhere quite distant from here), in an expedition financed by the Victor Heisenberg Gentlemen's Society. His purpose: to find clues of the existence of pre-*Homo sapiens* civilization in the deep desert.

"Richard!" you shout, grabbing him by his shoulders. "But how . . . what . . . what are you doing here? What happened to the expedition?"

"We saw it, we saw them," he mumbles. "Dear God, they are horrible! And what a level of perfection they reached in their civilization! They built this city from the ground and then lost it when the air on the surface became unbreathable, so full of that damned oxygen . . . They had to retreat to their underground caves, there where they were safe, where they could breathe their own air . . ."

"They? Who do you mean, those who built these statues for their gods?"

"These are no gods, you damn fool! The statues are a representation of themselves!" he shouts at you, completely deranged.

Turn to page 32

32

The old man breaks into a run, surprisingly nimble, and you struggle to keep up. You see how he slips through a fissure on the base of one of the columns that creates a cave.

"Here, here is where I found it . . . The biggest discovery of all . . ."

"What?" you ask him. "What was it that you found, Richard?"

"The pond! With meteorite water released by the old asteroids . . . Yes, the water that connects to your mind and predicts other times and other places . . . And also, the key, the accursed key! Forged with a meteorite mineral!"

He shows you a worn-out bag and produces a key from its inside. It's the oddest you've ever encountered, and its shape does not seem to fit the human hand. It's made of a material you fail to identify, but it shines lightly in the dark. The number 62 is etched on one of its sides. What could that mean?

The old man hands it to you, not with ease, but as if he is sharing something quite dangerous.

"Hide it. Hide it, I beg of you," he moans. "My strength is gone . . ."

"But what happened, Richard?" you ask, exasperated. "What happened to your colleagues? Did the bandits of the desert ambush you?"

The old man laughs; it's the tragic laughter of a demented mind. He shakes his head.

"No. Not bandits . . . Not even humans, no . . . It was *them.* I saw them coming in the water. But my colleagues wouldn't heed my words. They took me for a fool! Can you believe it?"

You shake your head, resigned.

You keep the key in your bag and turn to page 33

33

"Yes, they took me for a fool, but I saw it all in the water . . . I saw the images and I tried to warn them. In the end, they disappeared. Buried in the sand, swallowed by the music-from-below . . . and then there was only me. Good old Burton." A soft laugh escapes between the gaps in his teeth. "Only me."

"What damn pond are you talking about?"

He points at something down at the end of the cave. It looks like a baptismal font made of stone. A font whose antiquity numbs your senses. It's a piece of art that dates long before the myths of western man. It's full of a lapis-lazuli-colored liquid with extraordinary reflections rippling off of it – as if it were playing with the source of light.

"The water of dreams . . ." the old man murmurs with terror.

Will you look at it, trying to find whatever might have driven Burton insane? Or will you be more sensible?

If you look at the water, turn to page 98
Otherwise, turn to 89

34

According to your host, that medallion was found by his children near a depression in the soil a couple of miles northeast from here, in the Sun's Anvil – a despicable place for life and human sanity. You scrutinize the medallion that al-Fayid gifts you as a token of protection, and soon you feel that an unfathomable abyss of time stands between you and its origin.

You stare with horror at what it represents: a sort of hunched cross between human, reptile, and satyr, clad in a ritual robe. It holds some sort of impossible-to-describe artifact in its hands. But with a little imagination, it could be a futuristic gun taken from the fantasies of H. G. Wells or Jules Verne.

You thank him and tell him you'll depart the next day for the Sun's Anvil. Al-Fayid wishes you luck and tells you his children will escort you as far as they can, but they won't get near the valley of the Icewind Dale. When you ask him what that is, he answers with a shiver:

"The place where it's said that once stood the Nameless City." His gaze is fixed on you, as if judging whether you are fit to undertake such an adventure, and he speaks anew. He makes an odd, rising inflection at the end, as if somehow he is questioning you:

"Your dreams are pushing you too far, university man . . ."

Begin your journey to that faraway place on page 35

35

You leave the next afternoon, after the sun's strongest hours have passed. At midday, the temperature was around 130 degrees, but now it's down to a "pleasant" 105 degrees.

A couple of days after setting out with the merchant's children, a sandstorm catches you by surprise. There's something supernatural in the way it appeared out of nowhere. You hear odd voices swept by the wind, and beyond those . . . a melodic sound, something artificial, like a sort of alien music. Al-Fayid's children gesture protection with their fingers, and entrust themselves to Allah . . . but you doubt that any gods will have anything to do with this.

Hours later, the winds have separated you from your guides. You cry their names fruitlessly – in the middle of the tempest you can't even hear your own voice. You can't hear or see a thing, only the maelstrom of sand.

Will you meet your end here, in the middle of the most absolute nothingness?

In the air, quite distant, you can hear the abhorrent music again, almost as if it were a preternatural siren song . . .

Lost and scared, turn to page 68

36

In this long and narrow chamber that resembles an extension of the corridor, you see niches carved in the walls. They are lined with many wooden cases with glass fronts.

You walk up to them and examine them closely. They are oblong and horizontal, unsettlingly like coffins. An underground phosphorescence of mineral origin casts light on them – the same light that lets you see where you are going. Fantastic drawings compose a continuous mural, embellishments that one cannot simply describe. Clearly, they were not carved by human hands.

The coffins contain the mummified remains of abhorrent creatures whose ugliness stretches the limits of what any civilized mind could handle. They are reptiles mixed with dogs or hyenas and satyrs, with twisted horns and foreheads broader than Jupiter's. Their lack of a nose, their alligator-like jaws and hooked fingers . . . all these characteristics place them in a palaeontological category of their own.

But worst of all is that they wear rich clothing and ornamented jewelry. And that denotes advanced intelligence, which scares you the most.

Turn to page 38

The coffins contain the mummified remains of abhorrent creatures . . .

38

You stagger back, filled with terror, away from the cases with the corpses. But you can't get too far away from them because they are everywhere: stored on the floors, walls, and ceilings for the rest of eternity. Thousands upon thousands of mummified representatives of some ancient race.

The friezes on the wall show grotesque imagery, commentaries on the rites of a civilization that didn't believe in death (what old country does not have myths about the afterlife?), but which did perform sacrifices for their perverted gods. In one of the drawings you see a slender reptile clad in a robe, a sort of high priest, about to sacrifice a poor old man on an altar. The priest seems to be standing on top of a great pyramid or ziggurat at whose feet a great city full of slaves (humans, undoubtedly, the underlings of that abhorrent reptilian race) is spread out.

Suddenly, a noise startles you terribly: Something heavy has moved, making a din at the end of the corridor and casting a shiny golden light. It's as if one of the walls had detected your presence and opened up, like a great panel, so you could see what lies beyond.

Noises come from the back corridor as if something were coming your way. Something quite fast.

Turn to page 39

You are trapped between two unknown phenomena: Down one end of the corridor, there's an intense and mysterious light. It has an oddly artificial quality to it, so it can't be a window to the outside.

On the other end, there are those *things* coming toward you from the back corridor, cutting off your only exit.

If you decide to wait until whatever comes from the corridor catches up with you, turn to page 56

If, on the other hand, you resolve to go toward the light, run to page 69, fast!

40

What does Damascius have to do with the lost ruins of Araby? Could those pagan schools have gathered information that the Roman world, almost entirely Christian by then, condemned to death?

You found that there were excerpts from his main work, *Difficulties and Solutions of First Principles*, in Byzantine Patriarch of Constantinople Photious' Bibliotheca. That thread led you to those fragments, always seeking a match with those words in Arabic: "Nameless" and "City." After much sweating and some short trips to dirty, seldom-used libraries, you found it.

You managed to collect enough data to persuade the Advisory Board at the University that in a remote region in Araby there were rumors that from the sands rose the ruins of ancient buildings that were there before the arrival of Sabaeans migrants – the remnants of an archaeological site of immeasurable value whose adobe and stone buildings could be old enough to escape the memory of Thebes and Meroë.

Turn to page 41

41

You were exceedingly happy to be granted funding. Said and done, you came via New York – London – Cairo – Riyadh. And now, weeks later, here you are, about to die of hunger or thirst, willing to slit your camel's throat and eat him if that gets you a couple of extra hours, a short interval of survival with which to advance for another half a mile.

You are lost in the middle of somewhere the natives call the Sun's Anvil. Half a heartbeat away from starvation, your weak thoughts bring you back to the starting point of this adventure, your conversations with Baker and Armitage, and the corroded parchment. What a death trap you've walked into!

Suddenly, you discern some silhouettes on the horizon, above the dunes. It could be a mirage, another one . . . but it could also be men on camels. Peaceful merchants or cruel desert bandits? Who knows? You consider whether approaching them would mean your salvation . . . or your death sentence.

If you spur your camel toward those dark figures, turn to page 85
If you think it best to stay away from them, go to 8

42

You are spellbound by the unknown, the mysteries never before revealed to the human eye, not even in prehistoric times. And like the scientist you are, you can't avoid the calling, the enchantment. So you start descending, step by step, until the mist that seems to burn with that strange incandescence swallows you.

You wander for an indefinite amount of time between large structures, like the skyscrapers of New York, but whose shapes are the most grotesque you can imagine. There are many holes in these structures, but not a door or window to cover them. You see deformed sculptures representing the old gods (are they, though?), and machines that make impossible noises and tremble with pulsating vibrations, almost alive. Rather than electrical, they appear almost organic.

The neighbors' eyes are fixed on your body, but no one stops you. They let you walk with curiosity and never get in your way. You see them from afar, shapes through windows, furtive shadows slithering quite rapidly along the streets . . . but not one of them comes out in the open air (if you could even say that in such a big cavern).

Suddenly, the street you are walking along ends in an enormous square, some 1,600 feet wide. A building unlike any other towers over it.

A ziggurat.

Turn to page 43

43

You walk up the steps to the ziggurat, guessing (no, knowing!) that this is the same building that those beings painted on the walls. That's how you know that up there is an altar for human sacrifices. And that, inside the temple, there will probably be a high priest waiting, after years of silence, anxious to spill blood once again for his old gods. The blood of an American scientist from Miskatonic.

When you get to the top you see the altar, but also an object similar to a giant tuning fork, which plays the infamous music that is heard all over the valley. That sound is condensed in a visible haze of light, a sort of lightning, that goes through the ceiling of the cavern, always upwards, toward space.

A calling, perhaps? A distress message destined to find beings up there, in the firmament, that once lost the coordinates of earth's position? What will they do if they find it again, or if they intercept that lightning full of information, of pleas to the unnameable powers of the cosmic abyss?

The priest exits the temple, and he's holding something in his hands. A ritual knife.

He doesn't need to force you to lie on the sacrificial stone. Driven by insanity, you do it yourself.

THE END

44

"No!!" you scream with your new reptilian throat.

The other dragon men (that's the only name you can think of, although they might resemble hyenas crossed with giant Komodo dragons) stare at you, bewildered – bewilderment born out of amazement that degrades little by little into rage as they witness an act of heresy: how their high priest uses his sacrificial knife not to end the human's life, but to cut his ropes and run alongside him down the pyramid.

You don't make it very far because the terrifying blue rays of the alien machines catch you mid-run and vaporize you and the prisoner. But at least you die with some peace of mind: The horrible gods those monsters pray to won't have their snack today.

THE END

You try the lever, only to pull it out of its place. It was so rotten and fragile that you've broken it.

At least you did not activate any traps or have the ceiling fall on your head. That's some consolation . . .

Return to page 24 and choose another option

46

A primitive impulse leads you to walk toward the sandstorm, and you don't even know why. You cover your face with your turban and protect your eyes with the glasses bought in Cairo. The storm becomes a titanic, vertical wall of sand, full of violent whirlpools that swallow miles and miles of the desert with no mercy. Until it swallows you, too!

When high winds threaten to pin you against the ground and the sand particles pierce your skin like thorns, you start to think that this has been a mistake. Suddenly, you seem to see a dark figure in the middle of the haze, twice as tall as a human. It seems to stand on two feet, but something about it seems unreal, impossible . . . as if the symmetry of its body lacked any logic.

It might be a simple rock that the winds have eroded capriciously. Or a traveler on a camel fused into a single form that is confusing your brain. What will you do?

If you approach the shadow, turn to page 53
If you walk away from it, trying to get lost in the storm, go to 74

It's an insane and distressing idea! Abominable! To share a hideout with the mummy of a being that's been there, undisturbed, for thousands or perhaps millions of years!

But panic gives no good advice, and in these moments of need, of pure terror, you see no other or more obvious way out. So you force the coffin lid open. You lift it up and slide inside, not allowing your brain to think too much about what you are doing. Because otherwise, you'd start screaming in terror and your plan for hiding would be in vain.

The air trapped inside the coffin is . . . toxic. It burns your eyes and makes you sneeze. But even worse is how the creature feels to the touch; it literally crumbles into dust when you push it, as if it were made of sand. Its disintegration is sequential: first the clothes, now dried-up sheets; then the skin, a waterfall of pure sand; and lastly, the inner organs, which are horridly torn like little pieces of papier-mâché.

It's as if the creature were a long-forgotten and fragile dream that you destroyed with the touch of a finger.

Turn, anxious, to page 48

48

You keep silent track of the seconds as the reptiles approach your sarcophagus. They stare, scrutinize, smell the air threateningly . . . but they can't see you. They don't see you! Your strategy has been successful!

They walk past, thinking you've gone further down the corridor. After a long while, you leave your hideout between coughs, regretting having breathed half of that alien mummy's dusty body. Now it's in your lungs.

The time has come for you to return to the surface . . . or has it?

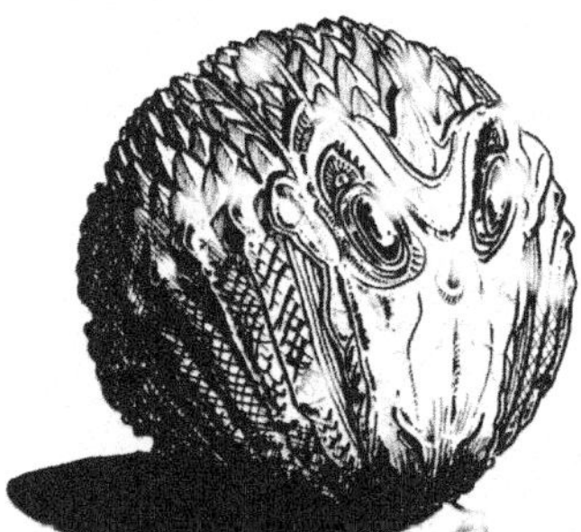

If you want to explore the luminescence at the end of the corridor after all, pluck up the courage on page 69

If you think it best to leave already, return to the surface, to the main city map on pages 102-103, and keep exploring

You decide the window is your best option. Climbing like a monkey, you sneak through the window to a small chamber, sheltered from the tempest.

The smell of warm food is the first thing you notice.

You are quite surprised to find two Bedouins around a fire made with sticks and camel dung. They are waiting for a piece of meat to be roasted. They are surprised to see you, but they don't get angry. They welcome you and invite you to sit down, so you also enjoy the rations.

In a corner of the room, you notice there's a pile of clothes – as if they belonged to a third person who is now absent. Maybe a change of clothes, or the belongings of someone who's gone naked into other parts of this same building?

The Bedouin men offer you a tasty blackberry juice that your dry throat receives kindly. It's delicious.

"What is this place?" you ask them in Arabic.

"Oh, this is the old temple, very old. For Ithaqua, the everlasting presence of the winds. The one who lives up there, next to the stars."

"Ithaqua?" you frown. "Doesn't ring any bells."

The two men sneer, and suddenly cold steel shines in their hands.

You are starting to feel dizzy. Could it be the blackberry juice?
Turn to page 51

The two men sneer, and suddenly cold steel shines in their hands . . .

51

Indeed, it appears that delicious juice had "something" in it. Some sort of sleeping venom that's paralyzing your muscles and blurring your vision.

One of the men unsheathes a sinister-looking knife, like the ones used for human sacrifice, as they shoot an incredibly evil smile at you.

"Ithaqua shakes the winds and whips the earth . . ." he tells you, hissing like a snake. "Overflies the sand deserts and frozen tundras from the confines of the earth where his lair is located. He needs to be calmed, and only human blood can do so. Another victim to sate his eternal hunger . . ."

Another? What does he mean? Come to think of it, those piled-up clothes of a third person . . . and that meat roasting in the fire . . .

God.
Holy God.
You're next.

THE END

52

When at last your eyes get used to the light, you realize you're in a chamber that's illuminated by an extremely odd machine: It looks like a metallic stalactite hanging from the ceiling, but it's half-made of crystal – several flashes of light slither like snakes along its length, creating the illusion of voltage discharge come to life. On the floor, right under the point of the stalactite, there's a chest containing a key of questionable design – it definitely wasn't made for the human mind.

The number 7 is etched on its bow. You pick it up and put it in your bag.

The corpses of these beings lie smoking on the floor. One of them has a helmet with wires that seem designed to connect their brain to the abhorrent machinery on the ceiling. For a moment, for a brief and delirious second, wild ideas of trying on the helmet and connecting your mind to alien technology cross your mind . . . But it's bound to be a bad idea. Not bad, terrible.

What will you do?

If you'd rather leave things as they are and not play around with technology you don't understand, return to the map of the city on pages 102-103 and keep exploring

If, on the other hand, your curiosity overcomes you and you want to try the helmet . . . suit yourself on page 97

53

Trying to master your fear, you walk toward the mysterious shadow until you can make out what it is: an ancient idol made of black stone that rises amidst the dunes, as if the wind had dug it up and was about to bury it again for another 10,000 years. Emerging from the sand, an unspeakable horror – the icon of an extinct civilization.

Looking at it, the idol inspires rejection and distress, for it doesn't resemble anything human. What sort of civilization would honor such a horrendous god? What s ort of insane cult could it generate?

The statue is tall and slender, two-legged like any human. But that's as far as similarities go. It has a reptilian head, the body of a hyena clad with ritual objects, and long draconian arms. Two satyr horns emerge from a forehead one would expect in a simian rather than an alligator.

Turn to page 55

Emerging from the sand, an unspeakable horror –
the icon of an extinct civilization . . .

You walk away from the idol, distressed. It rather looks like it's spent centuries, maybe even millennia, forgotten under the changing tide of the sand. In any case, its presence is so dreadful you'd rather get away as fast as possible, and you take to your heels.

Then you realize the high winds have not only dug up this statue, bringing it to light from its dusty tomb, but also another construction about a hundred yards from here: It looks like a temple with a pyramidal ceiling, made of the same black stone as the idol. It appears to have been constructed for war, not peace. A complex loop of wooden beams penetrates and emerges from its walls, like backstitches, strengthening it.

Since the storm doesn't seem to be dying down, you decide to seek shelter there before the winds end your life. Will you enter the temple through the ruined door or through a lateral window?

If you go through the door, turn to page 19
If you choose the window, go to 49

56

You hide behind one of the wooden cases that stick out of the wall, hoping to go unnoticed. The sounds seem like footsteps, and they are becoming heavier, like thunder. An inhuman, guttural moan accompanies the steps.

And then you see them.

At first there are three figures, shorter than a regular human but quite wide, as if they had dragon wings folded behind their deformed shoulder blades. It's them – the members of the ancient race that inhabited these chambers in prehistoric times. You can't tell now if they were awake or if it was your presence that brought them back to life, but there they are: moving, running, forming a crowd in the narrow corridor that leads to you.

What mysterious alchemy could have awoken them from dreams that spanned for centuries? Or worse still . . . could they be guardians of their kin, still dwelling in some secret sanctuary deep down, policing centuries of dreams? What will they do if they find you in their realm, a mere intruder that has come to violate their home?

Turn to page 57

Suddenly, you realize that your hideout is insufficient – you are certain these beings see in the dark better than you do. And besides, they look like they can trace smells with those snouts, so hiding from them will be quite difficult.

What to do? They are onto you!

If you decide to run toward the shiny light down the corridor, turn to page 84

If you desperately open the coffin next to you and squeeze in next to its "tenant," turn to 47

If somewhere along your journey you've found something that resembles an alien weapon, brandish it against these creatures on page 107

58

When you walk up to the structure that emerges from the dunes, you realize it's not only very tall and rectangular – but also quite narrow – thin, just like a wall. Or rather . . . a door.

The latter becomes more likely as you walk around it and examine it carefully. It looks like a bronze plate covered by layers and layers of caked sand. This antiquated relic is so immense that it defies any logical explanation for its size – this door that leads nowhere. It seems to be watching you – looking at you sideways from the primordial rocks and from the temples that surround the door like sullen watchmen.

There are carvings on the enormous bronze plate. As you scrutinize them, you try to draw them in your diary. You wonder what sort of archaic technology could not only carve but raise this metallic plate that must weigh a ton. Yes, the Egyptians did build the pyramids . . . but whoever built this bronze door possessed a knowledge that has been now lost.

The question that worries you the most: Why would one place a door in the middle of nowhere? Where did the builders think it would lead? Or is its origin symbolic, perhaps even religious or ceremonial, like the Celtic dolmens?

Turn to page 60

Where did the builders think it would lead?

60

A close examination of the engravings casts some light on the mechanism which, in theory, could open the large door. You find three holes concealed within the engravings which could be locks, each with a different shape. If you held all three keys, you could activate some sort of invisible mechanism that might well be concealed inside the structure of the door.

The question is: even if you managed to find the three keys and open it . . . Where will that get you if the door seems to lead nowhere?

Hidden in the Nameless City there are three keys. There is a different number etched on each of them. When you find all three, add the three numbers and go to the resulting page to open the Bronze Door. Until then, return to the main map on pages 102-103 and keep exploring.

61

A presence seems to stalk you from the ghostly rocks of the city. You try ignoring it as you walk to a double row of pillars that delineate a straight path, a road that wagons and people would have traversed in the old days. It would have been a sign of the prosperity of this place, now abandoned to who knows what horrible cataclysm.

From afar you discern a shape on top of each of the stone pillars, which rise at least 50 feet above the ground. You assume they might be the statues of old governors, like the ones crowning the peristyles of the Roman Empire. But as you get closer, you can make out more details . . . and what you see is deeply disturbing.

They are statues, but they don't represent human beings. Rather, they look like a cross of different animals: Two-legged and four-legged draconian reptiles mixed with satyrs, reminiscent of hyenas with broad foreheads . . . All of them in solemn poses, as if saluting days of glory now long gone. Are these gods, perhaps? Antediluvian myths turned to stone?

Suddenly, you hear a voice. A human voice. A man's. And it scares you almost to death.

Turn to page 63

Are these gods, perhaps?
Antediluvian myths turned to stone?

"You won't open it, you won't open it!" shouts the voice, scaring you almost to death.

You turn around and see a man come out from behind a column. He's old and his clothes are ragged; an unkempt and dirty beard hangs down his chin. The man runs to you and grabs you by your sleeve with pleading fingers. His vacant stare and trembling hands, unable to stay still for even a second, make you think the poor man must be insane.

"The Bronze Door must remain closed, whatever happens!" he shouts in a foreign accent. "I've looked at the Pond of Revelations and have seen what could happen if they cross the door to this world. You mustn't open it!"

"Who are you?" you ask him, trying to calm him down. You have the unpleasant feeling you know this man, and that you've seen him before in some faraway place.

"What are you talking about, sir? What door? And who are you?"

The old man's teeth chatter and an agonizing cramp seems to make all his muscles tense.

"The one that connects to the other city . . . The one Up Above. It must never be opened . . . Bury the keys, bury the keys!"

Turn to page 31

64

You walk up to a hole in the ground that's demarcated by eight segmented limestone walls. Each of them has a burr of stone sticking out, like a wave frozen in time, and is crowned by studs that resemble teeth. It looks like a disturbing, fang-covered mouth carved on the ground.

You stand near the edge and peek inside. It's a tunnel whose other extreme is lost in the depths of the earth, always shunning the sunshine, for never does the sun stand in such vertical alignment with this pit so as to illuminate its bottom. They were seeking the eternal night – total darkness for whatever dwells down there.

A night dial, instead of a sundial? Does darkness even set the time, some far-fetched lapse of time?

The metallic music you heard before comes, at least partly, from down here. Down there, deep down, there's something that produces that music when the wind sweeps past these galleries. You can't fathom what sort of artifact or alien musical instrument could make such a sound.

Turn to page 65

Suddenly, you notice something: Whenever the music plays, the wind sweeps sand down the tunnel and retrieves it later. You could jump inside with confidence, without risking your legs, if you just wait until the pit is exactly half-full of sand. Considering that in just one cycle it takes 17 hours for the wind to fill the tunnel with sand and another 17 to empty it, and that each hour it fills with twice the volume of sand of what there was before, at what exact time would you have to jump so that it is exactly half-full?

If you know the answer to the riddle, go to the corresponding page
Otherwise, return to the main city map on pages 102-103
and keep exploring

66

Your body is filled with an odd and irresistible force. You are no longer yourself; you are certainly not the George Aberdeen who left the United States to explore the most remote confines of the world (and look how far you've come!). Now you're another creature, another being. A tide of ideas, concepts, and feelings weakens your brain, as if radiating from some transmitter set right at the beginning of the Big Bang, with the birth of the universe. A horrible, titanic eye opens there, eclipsing half the sky with its radiance. It looks at you.

You raise your knife, possessed by willpower that is not your own, enslaved to the gods by the names no human throat could pronounce. The crowded square of the archaic city next to the ziggurat bursts into a deafening, fanatic screaming, chanting over and over again the names of their demented deities . . .

The knife plunges swiftly. One blow. Brutal and concise.

It's over for the victim.

But your living hell is just starting.

THE END

"No!" you scream, falling over the crest of the dune. You roll down the slope until you crash into a valley created between mountains of sand. You spit out dirt. You can't see a thing, and your bones hurt so badly you feel as though they've been hammered. And to top it all off, the layers of sand are burying you, threatening to suffocate you . . .

But you sit up. You stand up, displaying incredible willpower. You didn't come this far, half the world away from Miskatonic, to die buried in the sand.

There's no sign of the face chiseled by the wind. It disappears behind you – if it ever did exist . . .

And you're still alive. Lost, parched, but still alive after all. That's what matters.

Turn to page 68

68

You have no idea how many days the storm lasts, but you fancy it's an eternity. A terrifying eternity lost in the fog between walls of sand and dust one cannot cross and hurricanes whose friction burns your skin and guts and scratches the whites of your eyes like sandpaper.

Until, one day, it all vanishes. The wind dies down, the calm comes over, and the sun, at last, makes its way toward you, letting you enjoy the landscape that has unfolded around you.

The sight is breathtaking. You don't know to what remote confine of the desert you've made your way, but what's here almost stops your heart in awe.

You swallow. What could it be?

Hurry, go to page 100 to figure it out!

69

You approach the golden halo that seems to bathe the area as if you had walked into the sun's crown. It's hot, but it's inexplicably dry and cold.

And then, you let out a howl of deep and utter surprise.

You've just peered out to an infinite void of unlimited radiance, like the whole world might look when gazing down from the peak of Mount Everest – a sea of lustrous mist. It's as if the corridor ended in such a gigantic underground cave that its limits exceeded your range of vision and are blurred in the frontiers of that ominous radiance.

There's no doubt there's something down there. Something that makes incomprehensible noises and that mysterious music you've been hearing all along. Mental associations are curious, and you shrink with fear at the idea that, except for the poor human figure destined for sacrifice that you saw on the friezes, you are the only human form amidst relics and symbols of primordial life.

Astounded, turn to page 70

70

There are winding stairs that go down into the depths of the world, and which may lead to the base of this titanic cavern. The abyss poses a dilemma for even a feisty explorer: Go down and stare at those marvels with your own eyes, even if it damages your sanity . . . or backtrack as fast as possible, before some nameless beings notice you?

Not even the physical horror of your situation when contemplating such a vast panorama, this world full of spectral mist, could compare to the feeling of surveying the archaic scenery, so huge it changes your perspective. Here, time itself has become the guardian of nameless and profane secrets.

Then a hurricane-force gale pushes you off your feet and hurls you downstairs. It causes a cacophony so loud that it makes your skull vibrate. You scream in pain, hugging the sides of your head so it doesn't burst, and you fall.

Roll to page 78

You think you've guessed right; when you pull the lever, a secret lateral passage opens up to your left. It leads you to the outermost core of the building. You find the low ceilings claustrophobic, and they leave you distressed.

You got it right! Of course, the result was the number of circles or zeros in each one. There are six circles in 09086 if you count the two there are in the 8, so the right answer is six.

You walk with extreme care in the dark. The moon is visible through a skylight. It seems to be shaking, as if reflected in a pond of quivering waters. For some unknown reason, you find the sight comforting – even though you feel more scared than words could tell . . . although not enough to quash your thirst for wonders.

This new George Aberdeen that ventures into the deepest chamber of the building is no longer your old, shy self, but a feisty explorer like the ones who filled in the gaps of all the empty maps of Africa . . . and he heads for the deepest chamber of the temple.

What will he find?

Turn with courage to page 72

72

The chamber it leads to is wide and circular, and there don't seem to be any windows. Not even in past times, when the desert hadn't buried it yet, did it have any ventilation. Vestiges of old paintings cover the walls, curious wavy lines whose paint has peeled off.

And in the center of the great chamber . . .

There's a pedestal, and on it, a key. At least, it looks like a key, although the shape of the bow suggests it wasn't made for a five-fingered hand.

You walk to it with its golden shimmer (for it seems to be carved out of gold) glittering in your eyes. A feeling of cruel greed numbs your senses. Is this how Sir Allan Quatermain felt when he saw Solomon's treasures in the depths of Africa for the first time?

The number 37 is etched on one side of the key.
What could this mean?
There's nothing left to explore here. Keep the key in your pocket and return to the main map of the Nameless City on pages 102-103 and pick another destination

73

Desperate, you produce the alien weapon from your bag and aim it at that thing. You're glad you brought it along, although you have no idea if it'll work.

When the monster is about to jump on you, its deformed mouth completely open and oozing a slimy drool, you pull the trigger. To a chant of "Abhoth, Abhoth!" the creature shrinks and expands, trying to move sideways. It's as if it could tell somehow that what you're holding is exactly what you think it is, and it tried to dodge the ray that's about to come out of the muzzle.

But it can't. When you shoot it, a circular field, 5 1/2 feet in diameter, lights up, encapsulating the creature and evaporating every last molecule of water in its body. The thing dies, becoming a thin mass of sand. You stare at your gun in terror, wondering what would happen if you shot a human with it. Do you really want to bring it back to civilization?

Climb with determination to page 24 and choose another option

74

A deep shiver overpowers you. You can't tell what that thing is and you're not sure what would become of you if you dared to look at it from a closer distance, but it gives you a bad feeling. There's something supernatural about it, something that gives you the feeling that you should get as far away as possible, begging for your life and trying to find the way back to civilization.

You won't do the latter, but you think it reasonable to leave there as soon as possible. Violent fragments of stories from the *Livre d'Ivon* burst into your mind. These stories feature wind spirits which only possess a body as long as it is embraced by these sandy maelstroms. Evil spirits that, according to certain pagan myths, are the wandering souls of travelers who've vanished in the vast desolation of the desert and now haunt it – riding ghostly camels, always in search of new prey to slowly torture.

You don't know which way to flee, though. In the eye of the storm, there are no directions, just uncharted regions. You tremble, tired and uncertain, and venture further and further into the hurricane.

Turn to page 75

75

Time loses its value, and soon your notion of the passing of each minute (let alone the hours) becomes unclear. The storm howls like an appalling beast around you, as if alive and driven by a dark will.

At some point during this torment, you fancy seeing an enormous figure in the whirlpool, chiseled by the winds on the cliff of sand – it is (or it resembles) a human face, with something like immense eyes that stare at you from the sky. A protuberance right below them could be the nose, and the grotesque outline of a mouth, a horizontal cut in the blizzard of sand.

"Dear Lord!" you scream in terror, and the rational part of your brain fights to stay sane. An optical illusion, that must be it, of course! "Don't be scared!" your inner self tells you.

But you can't help it. Reason becomes powerless here – an overwhelming sense of dread seizes you as you sense the large face bearing down on you.

If you raise your hands, offering yourself to it, just in case it turns out to be an old spirit from the desert, turn to 4

If you roll down the dune like a dead body, relying on pain and inertia to take you away from there, go to 67

The two of you are paralyzed, eyes fixed on each other. Neither can blink. A moment later, he extends a kind hand and invites you to sit on a stool by his side. Dazed, unsure how to react, you obey.

You almost have a heart attack when the being slowly moves his mouth, as though trying to accommodate his tongue to sounds it wasn't designed to produce, and he speaks in a sort of protohistoric Sabaean language:

"Man-from-up?"

You don't understand him at first, but then he points a finger with a broken nail to a nearby helmet. You put it on . . . and the language becomes comprehensible in your head!

"You shouldn't be here. This is no place for your people," he rasps. "The fungi from Yuggoth should not have let your race prosper. They are our friends."

"Uh . . . I came here by accident," you mumble in that forgotten tongue. "Wh-what are you? Why are you here?"

"No. The question is, why are you here," the old man mutters. "You are impossible. We are as we were millions of years ago."

He's right. You'd never thought about it that way. It's you, the human race, who climbed down from trees and lost your body hair.

"I'm the Chronicler. I observe, date, and write. I'll write your visit, too, so that the memory of this day is not lost in Eternity."

Turn to page 79

77

Things didn't end up well, my dear friend.

If you're reading this page, it means the horrors and secrets you found in your adventure became too much for you. Your poor, rational, Western mind was not able to resist the exposure to such scenes, and you've gone insane! You'll spend the rest of your days in a padded cell in an asylum, I'm afraid. But don't worry, there are very nice people there to take care of you, and who'll make sure you have everything you need. And if they don't heed your mumbles and warnings? Well, they'll get it when the time comes. When the secrets are revealed, the whole planet will learn you were right and that the terrifying marvels you encountered were real.

As a sick mind once said: "The most merciful thing in the world is the inability of the human mind to correlate all its contents. We live on a placid island of ignorance in the midst of black seas of infinity . . ."

THE END?

78

You roll uncontrollably down the stairs, hurting yourself all the way to the landing of the long staircase, a place where five or six other branches open up – all of them winding, twisted, and difficult to maneuver.

Holding your head where the fall cut your scalp (thankfully, it isn't too deep), you look around. You shudder because, from this distance, you can make out the shapes inside the radiance: sharp tips of stone that come out of a sort of haze; vertical slabs full of small windows that resemble inhabited obelisks; shadows of large constructions in the shape of bridges; and small flames of combusting gases that twisted chimneys exhale.

It's a city, but it's not a human city. That's for certain. And there seem to be inhabitants.

The closest building to you is like a pagoda, except the eaves of the roofs are upside down. And the door is open, as if the owners don't mind anyone coming in. Actually, it seems there are no windows or doors anywhere, only holes in the walls.

If you head toward that first building to explore it, turn to page 93
If you keep walking down the stairs to the deep city, go to 42

79

"How is it you're still alive, hidden in the depths of the world?" you ask the Chronicler.

"At first, there was heat and gas, primordial fire, whole continents of melting lava. Then it rained for millions of years and your oceans came to be. The air on the surface turned unbreathable and we had to lock ourselves down here. We, who were once strong and mighty. Who once ruled the world . . . hidden, hidden like the horned viper. Humiliated, unable to live under the cruel sunlight."

The old man appears quite sad and melancholic, as if remembering the days he himself lived as a child. But that's impossible. Is he suggesting his race is immortal? Is that why there are no references to the afterlife in their friezes?

"But we've worked – oh, yes, we have – patiently, with the aid of our brothers, the Yuggoth . . . They possess the knowledge, they fly over new pastures where the damnable oxygen is not an issue. The New City is almost completely finished. Down here, there are but a few of us . . ."

"Wh-what new city? Where have you built it?"

The creature takes some time to react, but he ends up looking up at the ceiling. And you realize that his stare alludes to a place in that direction, very far up. Maybe beyond his cavern. Maybe up above the world at the surface. Maybe beyond the clouds.

Turn to page 80

80

The Chronicler is absorbed by his engravings and doesn't say a word. You set the translating helmet in its place and leave the room, crestfallen. What he's told you has left you deeply disturbed.

Before leaving, you take a key that is hanging from a thin chain. The number 7 is engraved on one of its sides. You keep it in your bag and retrace your steps to the surface, lost in monstrous thoughts.

Return to the general map of the city on pages 102-103 and keep exploring

81

You pull the wrong lever. You know this instantly because a pit opens at your feet and you fall into a hole surrounded by masonry walls. It's perfectly cubic and presents no exits. Landing hurts, but luckily you haven't broken anything.

Then you look around, and what you see curdles your blood.

You are not the first (nor probably the last) one to fall through one of the many traps in these buildings. Maybe the architects built them with the same purpose in mind as those who built the pyramids in Egypt – that is, to ward off grave robbers. And sure enough, they proved effective!

The floor is full of skeletons, mostly human . . . although there are some you fail to identify. You'd guess they belonged to some sort of animal, but who could tell? Is this your destiny?

You are still wondering about this when the Thing leaves its hole and looks at you with a multitude of shiny eyes.

Turn to page 82

82

Terror cramps your limbs. Upon seeing that creature, the most ancient human fear – the fear of being eaten by a predator – comes fresh and stinging to your brain, paralyzing your very last muscle.

What escaped the niche in the wall is a complex being, albeit deformed to a level your brain struggles to comprehend. It's an abomination that could well be the amputated limb of another larger abomination, for that's what it looks like – a piece of a body, and not a body on its own, as if it were but a living and moving arm or leg.

There's no doubting its hunger and the fact that it can crawl toward you by contracting its deformed body. Each time it contracts, it adopts a horrible shape – although not as bad as when it stretches. A mass of glutinous polyps burst open, one at a time, from its sides, revealing a darkened bubble that might well be its eye, and an injury becomes unsewn just beside it, exposing its guts to the humid air, imitating a mouth.

"*Abhoth, Abhoth!*" it screams.

It can talk! That denotes intelligence, even if rudimentary. The scientific side of your brain starts wondering as you slowly back up and flatten yourself against the wall.

Turn to page 83

83

Desperately, you reach for your equipment bag. With a leap that defies its physiology, this creature lands before you, right in the middle of the pile of human bones. A stinking green drool oozes from its gaping mouth, and upon touching the bones, they dissolve, as if the substance were a sort of organic acid.

Trembling in fear, you stick your hand in your bag, hoping to find something useful.

If you have found an alien object similar to a gun or rifle in your adventures, turn to page 73

If you want to use your light burner, go to page 25

If you'd rather pick up a bone and use it as a mace, go to 18

84

Seized by fear, you flee toward the light-dominated space, fancying it might be a passageway to somewhere. A lucky exit to the outside world.

Sadly, you never reach it. The sound of something like energy gathering in a collector comes from behind you, and when these energies are released, you're in their way.

Disintegration is still an unknown word at the time. At least for ordinary people, although not for scientists like Albert Einstein – already working on the mysteries of the atom. But that doesn't mean you can't suffer it.

THE END

You approach the men, if that's what they are. Now you just need to figure out if they are friendly, or if they belong to those dangerous tribes of desert bandits you've been warned of.

They look sullen and threatening, and when they see you coming they ready their guns just in case you're a threat. But you, who know the customs of the Bedouin people, call upon *diyafa*, the principle of hospitality among travelers. They eye you suspiciously but agree to your accompanying them to their camp, which is no farther than a six-hour-long journey. You sincerely thank them and, when asked why you've come to such a place, you tell them about your quest to find the Nameless City.

Hearing this, you notice them tense ever so slightly. They exchange knowing looks but remain quiet. You ask them what is wrong, whether you've unknowingly made a faux pas, but they just offer you a sip of water. They watch you with analyzing eyes, as if one of you were keeping a terrible secret.

Their campsite, a group of tents sheltered behind a dune, appears just moments later. You see more men and women, as well as camels; a settlement of travelers that has decided to camp here today.

Turn to page 87

Al-Fayid shows you a relic from a distant and obscure past.

A man who introduces himself as Laksi al-Fayid, the patriarch of the clan, invites you to his tent and shares his food. This is a great honor, and you are very grateful. When you tell him what you came to the desert to find, he's dumbfounded.

"The Nameless City is a ghost from the past," he tells you. "One you should not awake. There are dark and obscure rumors about that place."

"But does it really exist? Have you seen it?" you ask, hopefully. Even if they don't want to take you there, they could give you some directions.

"I advise you to forget it, honored sir," he says in a pleading voice. "Dark legends mention a place on earth made not for men, and which stood there long before we came . . ."

"Before who came?"

"Humans."

The flames crackle in the fire. An odd wind shakes it.

"But . . . there are writings that speak of it. I have read an old Arab poet, Abdul Alhazred . . ."

When he hears that name, al-Fayid tenses as if bitten by a snake.

Turn to page 88

88

"Don't you dare speak that accursed name in my home!" he shouts, as he gestures to protect himself from the Evil Eye. "It's not a good memory, nor someone worth summoning."

"I'm sorry," you apologize, blushing. Why the hostility? "I didn't know he was considered persona non grata here."

"Mad poet, voice of the dead, and the abyss of madness and dementia . . . That sick madman dared to travel to prohibited places and composed his poems and wrote his accursed books honoring the horrors he encountered there . . . He was an ungodly man." He shudders.

"Did he know the location of the lost city?"

"Yes, and it was there, in those old, dusty streets, where he composed his most famous verse."

"Which one?"

In a low voice and with an odd glimmer burning in his eyes, he recites it:

"That is not dead which can eternal lie, and with strange eons even death may die . . ."

He shows you an old medallion. The void of time that separates you from it shakes you to the core.

Impressed, go to page 34

89

"I don't think this is a good idea," you tell Burton. But then you see a change in his eyes. His gaze becomes even more lost and dangerous.

"You won't shame the Old Ones . . . I'm telling you to stare into the water!" he cries.

You step back, raising your hands. You don't want to hurt him, but he might even hurt you in a fit of dementia.

"Listen, Burton, you are sick. Let me help you. Together we can find a way out, and then we will return to Cairo for backups. The Victor Heisenberg Society will provide us with all the supplies and human equipment we request."

"I told you to stare at the water!" he howls, and lunges at you like a furious tiger.

The wretched old man's strength is surprising – he immobilizes you, grabbing you by the arms and twisting them to your back. He presses your face against the basin. You almost lose a tooth to the impact. You try wriggling yourself free, but it's impossible. Burton seems to possess a superhuman strength, something unnatural!

Unable to stop him, he violently turns your head so it faces the water. Your eyes are fixed on the liquid where some flashes dance . . .

Turn to 90

90

Those flashes drag you psychically, stealing your soul and submerging it in a vortex of lights, feelings, and darkness, all at the same time. You see what drove Burton insane, scenes of bloody sacrifices – human sacrifices – and nameless gods. Ten million years ago, stuck between old dates and cataclysms and the dawn of humanity.

You see the race that put up a fight to abandon the stages their bodies had known for such a long time, places where they'd settled in like nomads during the youth of the earth. When you think you can't take it any longer, you see their god, you get a glimpse of that presence: an incredibly evil being who lurks in the shadows of the depth of the cosmos . . . and your sanity snaps. With a unique and clean snap. Nothing makes sense to you anymore. The sight of that Great Old One is too much for your weak creed. You go as insane as old Burton.

Months later, you are found wandering on your own in the desert. A group of fishermen finds you. They bring you back to the States via the American embassy in Cairo. Unlucky for you, there's not much of you left. At least concerning sanity.

Turn to page 77

91

You reach a plain where the sand deposited by the wind seems to conceal an old painting. Below the large deposit of yellow dust, straight, dark lines show here and there.

You walk in ever-broader circles, like a cartographer setting the limits of geographic landmarks. An hour later, you're reasonably confident that the shape drawn by those concealed lines is that of a nine-point star. And in at least two points, there is an ingress: cracks that might well have served as sewers in a distant past where there was water to drain.

What could be the meaning of these lines? Is it a religious or purely ornamental meaning . . . or maybe something more practical? You've recently heard about a great finding in South America, where there are large lines that popular imagination has turned into landing strips for the carriages of gods . . . but you don't know if this is the same thing. Besides, what sort of forgotten gods would want to land here?

Determined to investigate, you slip through one of those sewers. It's a long and narrow pipe whose walls, despite the desert's heat, still retain some lucky, dormant humidity – a fossilized but watery dampness.

Turn to page 92

92

You descend further into darkness, to the most remote depth, where the unexpected wind that brings the metallic, inhuman music that has had your hairs on end seems to emanate.

Suddenly the tunnel opens into a domed gallery that ends in an ugly flight of stairs. They are small and steep and will give you nightmares for the rest of your life, for you'll come to learn what they are for – and who treaded them long ago. The ceiling is also quite low, uncomfortable even for an average man like yourself.

In the dark, as the tunnel becomes narrower and more cramped, gems of wisdom from your demonic books come to mind. Like the words the demented Alhazred once wrote: "That is not dead which can eternal lie, and with strange eons even death may die." But not only this, but also fragments from Damascius' heretical works, and infamous sentences from the delirious *Image du Monde* by Gauthier de Metz.

Are you hallucinating? Has the darkness of the underworld overpowered you?

All of a sudden, the tunnel opens into a bigger chamber, full of odd objects.

Crawl through the tunnel to page 36

93

Why didn't the architects need doors? Perhaps if you live in the Underground City you are trustworthy? No one sneaks down here uninvited; every building belongs to every inhabitant? Maybe the very concept of property hasn't been invented.

The main door leads to a circular chamber with abhorrent decoration, full of objects whose purpose your mind cannot grasp. It could be a sort of storeroom, or even a museum . . . or simply the home of one of those creatures, filled with the objects they collect throughout their lives.

A noise comes from the upstairs floor. A sort of cough or guttural grunt; you couldn't tell. There's a staircase, with the same small, low steps you've grown used to, that ascends in a spiral. Trying to make as little noise as possible, you climb the steps one at a time until your head pokes out on the landing and you see what's up there.

You hold your breath.

Turn to page 94

94

This second floor looks like a study room – the walls are covered in cupboards and there's a large, low desk in the center. An inkstand? The cupboards are full of seemingly quite thin and half-transparent obsidian sheets. Each has an irregular outline that's different from the rest. They are full of cuneiform doodles whose internal symmetry resembles some sort of writing. But there are also drawings that look more like technical diagrams than artistic expressions, surrounded by dots and grooves.

But what catches your attention the most is the creature that sits before the inkstand.

It's one of those creatures, a cross between a hyena, a reptile, and a Greek mythological creature. It appears very old and decrepit, and it's much more hunched than the ones you've encountered so far, as if its body were hanging from its arched spine.

It's carving a sheet of obsidian with what appears to be an instrument that works with heat. What sort of incredible knowledge is this creature recording for posterity?

Slowly, the Chronicler spins his chair and looks at you.

Turn to page 76

You keep the artifact in your bag (it could have an incalculable archaeological value if you manage to bring it back to civilization) and resolve to abandon the temple.

You examine the walls. Splendid and vigorous drawings, boldly fantastic, create a continuous mural that snakes its way through walls and ceiling. Unless your eyes deceive you, they represent half-man, half-dinosaur creatures that witness key moments of history that are not recorded in the annals of Christianity. Does that mean they are from an earlier time, like that fireball falling from the skies? Or those splitting plates whose silhouettes vaguely resemble America and Africa?

For the love of God, what historic period do these murals represent?

Turn to page 96

96

You find a passageway concealed in the mural. It's narrow and it leads upstairs, all the way to the surface. You end up back in the desert right when the sandstorm seems to have died down. You pluck up your courage and leave, praying you'll make it to some inhabited place.

During the first day, the storm subsides to nothing but a mildly annoying breeze. And the damnable artifact weighs a ton in your bag. But then, that very same night, the cruel wind resumes its blowing.

And you get lost again in the immensity of the sand, not knowing where your feet are leading you . . .

Wander to page 68

97

It was a bad idea. You acknowledge it as soon as the energies establish a connection between the mass of neurons in your brain and the labyrinth of protons and electrons that inhabit this stalactite.

What's the price of knowledge? What would a good scientist give for absolute power, for seeing with their own eyes and comprehending with their developed mind the mysteries of the Universe? When the alien machinery links your mind to the archive of knowledge of this ancient race, your neurons die, but for a brief instant you are the happiest man on earth. Because you know EVERYTHING. You hold all the answers to every enigma of the universe.

The problem is that the volume of information is too much for you, and although it doesn't kill you, it casts your psyche into a demented abyss that it cannot escape.

Turn, sadly, to page 77

98

Somewhat reluctantly, you inch toward the water. The liquid reflects the light in a thousand asymmetrical prisms.

Leaning over the basin and looking inside, something incredible happens.

At first it's just a change in color, as if the liquid knew someone or something was staring and it was reacting to the contact of the observer. But then it starts bubbling, which is odd since there is no heat, and then it bursts into images, violent waterfalls of unmoving pictures, so that you cannot really tell whether you are actually seeing them or if they are in your mind.

Burton laughs behind you.

"Another witness of the great revelation! Oh, my God, another witness!" he cries, shooting his arms into the air. "Show him the Truth, you magnanimous beings! Show him the Truth, so that he is aware too, and ready for the upcoming times!"

His demented tirade goes on, but you are no longer listening. Your gaze is fixed on the images displayed by the water. And they are the most terrifying things you've ever seen.

Because you see them. And, in return, they see you too.

You see the reptilian creatures clad in shapeless rags, building temples, making this city. When did this happen? One hundred, two hundred thousand years ago? Ten million, perhaps?

Turn to page 99

99

You see them using some strange machinery to lift large rocks and place them one on top of the other. It's a purely theological society, based on the compliance of rituals and cults for nameless deities. It's the chronicle of a mighty seacoast metropolis that ruled the world before Africa came out of the waves. You see their wars and triumphs, their tribulations and defeats. You see them eventually retreating to the depths when the air became unbreathable for them. Digging, digging in search of the world their prophets spoke of . . .

They are down there. Underground. Still.

When the vision dissolves, you see Burton's body by your side – he's dead. He's left you alone again. But at least you've got the key.

Once you've buried him, you return to the city map on pages 102-103

100

The sun is a bucket of blood and the horizon is a taut wire. Just as you have exhausted your strength and you feel like you are about to pass out, the storm starts to die down and the gray horizon turns to a roseate light edged with gold.

Then you see it, and at first you think it's a mirage caused by your fevered state.

Shapes, shapes emerging from the sand, covering many square miles of desert far and wide. Edges of rocks, dense dark masses that can only be buildings, apertures of very different shapes like wells on the ground, leading to who knows what untrodden depths . . .

It's a city. Or what's left of it after being buried for thousands of centuries at the mercy of sandstorms. Could it be the lost city of the legend, the one without a name? Have you finally found it? It's possible, although at this moment you even question your own sanity.

Suddenly, a loud metallic peal is heard in the valley. Music – cosmic, outlandish, ominous sounds, unlike anything any human mind has ever composed! A draft of air that resembles the moans of a living creature comes from one of those openings on the ground, from some remote depth. What could it be?

What evil creature or musical instrument was cursed with a throat that could produce such a sound? Trying to fight off the fear, you set out for the valley where the city has emerged, hoping you'll never know the answer . . .

Turn to page 101

101

You wander between brooding ruins of houses and buildings, unable to find inscriptions or friezes that mention men. You fail to see any allusions to the old civilizations we know of, like the Egyptian or Mesopotamic. How could this be? What sort of civilization doesn't sculpt their fate, or their myths, so that they survive the trap of time?

You can't see any logic in this morbid architecture, nor the smallest proof that this had been built by human hands. Even some proportions in these buildings make you feel uneasy. There are no bystanders but the wind – a wind that is old as time – that blows between the rocks and the white moon that rises like a naked bone.

You start exploring the city, praying you won't find something your brain won't be able to take . . .

Well, traveler, you've found the Nameless City! Congratulations! Or should we say . . . condolences? Examine the map on pages 102-103. There you'll find the buildings are numbered. These are the pages you can jump to as you explore the city little by little. Don't lose sight of this map – you can always come back to it to explore another building. And good luck! The ancient enigmas of the Nameless City await you . . .

10
64
91
58

You've found the Nameless City!

104

You point at one of the walls carefully, holding the artifact with both hands. Is this how you use it, or are you holding it backwards? Who knows what will happen when you press that button? Maybe it'll play music. Maybe it'll open a portal to a strange and distant place. Maybe nothing will happen.

Screwing up your face, you hold it as far away as possible and press the button. At first, nothing happens. But slowly, a vibration makes it shake in your hands as it heats up. Then something does happen – before you, on the wall, a circle the size of a horse is drawn. Then the rock cracks and small currents of dust are formed and vacuumed to the center of this symmetrical disc, where it gathers and forms a sphere of burnt-out mass.

When it ends, there's a hole that leads to the outside desert. But there hasn't been heat or noise or movement in the air. It's been a slow molecular disintegration of inert matter.

What an atrocious weapon! What sort of civilization could create such a thing, and with what purpose?

Turn to page 105

105

You decide to take the object with you, not so much owing to its hole-opening capabilities, but to its incalculable historical and archaeological value. Futuristic technology built and designed thousands of years ago – who would believe that? Your peers from the University will be speechless.

In a better mood, and seizing the moment when the storm seems to have died down a little, you step into the desert in search of another place for shelter. This building that you've found is the undeniable proof that the Nameless City you were so eager to find does really exist. The mythical lost city from those legends! Could you find any more buildings, or is this the only one that the storm has dug up?

Pluck up your courage as your wander to page 68

106

You've managed to find the three keys . . . amazing! Crawling in exhaustion, with joints burning in pain and fatigue, you near the large door and stick each key in its socket. Since they are very different in size, shape, and weight, it's not hard to find which belongs where.

When you're done, you turn them in the opposite direction from the movement of the sun. That's bound to have some mysterious meaning somewhere. The large bronze plate moans and trembles as if alive . . . The carvings on the door, showing seas and continents whose names humans have forgotten, break down into thin cascades of dust.

You step back, frightened, when you see that a thin slit of light has snapped the plate in two right down the middle. But it's not any ordinary light, and that's what scares you the most – it looks like a luminescence that's been stolen from another sun. Light from other times, irradiated in past geological eras that were yet to succumb to decay. The door trembles and opens at last, after keeping a silent watch for thousands of years.

The door opens before you. Turn to page 109 to discover what awaits on the other side

107

You can't escape, there's no time to think. You must defend yourself!

You produce the odd-looking weapon from your bag, and with the stance of a warrior, you stand in the middle of the corridor, right before the creatures, aiming at them.

The three lizard-like beings come to a halt, taken aback. Obviously, they didn't anticipate a human being standing up to them, let alone with one of their antediluvian artifacts. They exchange looks and then turn around and flee down the corridor, howling grotesquely.

With a cry of rage, you run after them with your weapon at the ready. You turn many corners, always going down, until another incredibly bright light blinds you. They must have opened a door that leads to the same illuminated space as the one you can access from upstairs, whatever that is. They've escaped through that!

"Aaaaaah!" you yell as you follow the creatures like a demented man.

Turn to page 108

108

You step through a door that leads to an interior chamber – into a nimbus of golden light. Blinded as you are, you struggle to make out some shapes fluttering in the air before you. What could they be?

Suddenly, loud bangs shake the rock around you. They are shooting! Those beings also have guns, and they are using them against you. You barricade yourself beside the gate and fire back, making your gun sing and vibrate with unnameable energies between your fingers.

The following minutes are a berserk rendition of the gunfight at the O.K. Corral. The half-liquid whoosh of the release of energies swamps the air while violent explosions peel off the stone walls.

Finally, you're the last one standing. The corpses of these reptilians are shapeless, smoking masses on the floor. Good shooting!

And your eyes, at long last, adjust to the light.

Turn to page 52

109

The door opens ominously. But what's on the other side doesn't correspond to the reality of your world. It's not the desert that one would reasonably expect to find; it's not even part of the Nameless City.

What the door reveals is a nimbus of golden light, a path to some other place. A tunnel made of light that leads to undreamt places. And, like the scientist you are, you surprise yourself by putting one foot in front of the other and inching your way to the large, shining rectangle.

Until it swallows you.

How do you convey a trip to infinity in words? A change of reality and paradigm? There might not be a language that adheres to such realities, but your eyes see it – your brain absorbs a torrent of colors, odd geometries, and wild dimensions.

When it's all over, you are on the other side, standing before a new landscape, a world that is alien to you. Suddenly, your presence catches the eye of the *things* that inhabit it. The door, needless to say, closed behind you.

Now it is impossible to return to your world. Your only option is to go on.

Turn to page 111

As a scientist, you wonder if you've gone too far this time . . .

111

An obviously lunar landscape welcomes you, not unlike the earth's moon, with its craters and smooth mountains of fine white dust. In the middle stands a city that mirrors what you knew in your time as the Nameless City, but splendid and majestic, in full bloom. You see it full of short, industrious beings, busy with their chores, who spread their wings and fly toward you when they spot you, as if asking themselves who the intruder might be. And the strangest thing is that the lack of air doesn't kill you. You are still alive, still breathing, as if the pressure of an invisible dome that covered the whole crater were able to maintain the basic conditions for life inside it.

The sky is teeming with asteroids. There are luminous cities in some of them, shining with a million pin-pricks of light. Inhabited. You can't tell whether you are in an incredibly remote past or in a distant future in which the moon has broken into pieces and formed a ring around its mother planet. A ring where these things, these beings, have finally succeeded in building their own ideal civilization.

As a scientist, you might have gone too far, even for the most extreme frontiers of science . . .

THE END

DRAMATIS PERSONAE

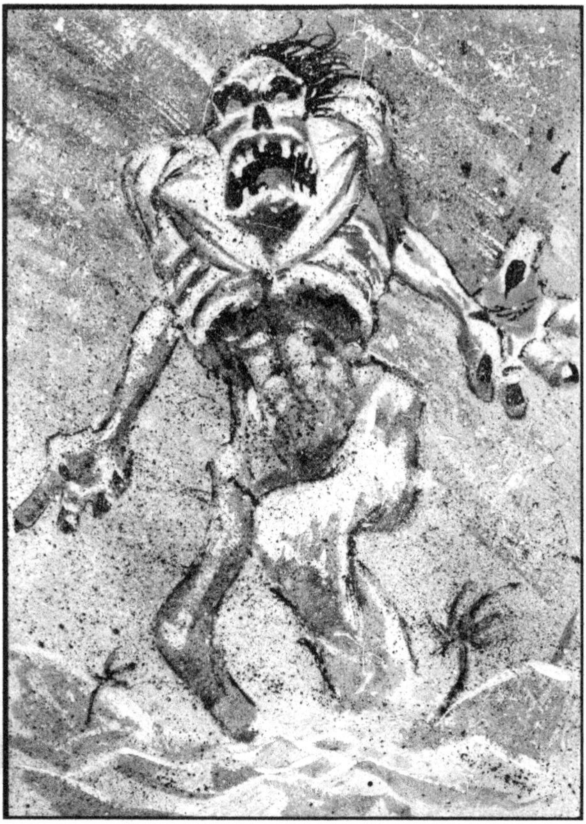

Ithaqua

One of the Great Old Ones, he appears as a horrifying, deformed giant with a roughly humanoid shape and glowing red eyes. He is usually spotted around Arctic regions, where Native Americans and Inutos have had the misfortune to encounter him.

He is believed to prowl the desolate North Pole in search of prey, hunting down any living thing in the most gruesome fashion. Since many legends associate him with the legend of the Wendigo, it is possible he uses the wind to whisper to the hopeless to move from the safety of the paths and follow him.

His nickname, Wind-Walker, suggests that where there is an intense enough draft, he can be summoned.

Abdul Alhazred

A poet of Sanaá, in Yemen, circa 700 A.D. He was known for his frequent visits to the lost cities of antiquity, such as Babylon and the subterranean secrets of Memphis in Egypt. He spent 10 years alone in the great southern desert of Arabia, which is believed to be inhabited by demons and creatures from unknown dimensions. In 730 A.D., he returned to civilization and, while living in Damascus, wrote the book of Ultimate Evil, *al Azif*, or, as it was known later, the *Necronomicon*.

Either in 731 or 738 (the date is uncertain, according to biographers), then known as the Mad Arab, he disappeared from the face of the planet – although some claim that his tomb lies in the Nameless City that exists within the Roba el Khaliyeh desert.

Great Race of Yith

Creatures capable of traveling through time that inhabited the earth in the distant past. They lack a physical body and resort to possessing those they wish to inhabit.

Djinni

Plural of djinn. Minor desert demons featured in Arab legends. They have power over sandstorms and other phenomena of the deep desert.

Wind

In the most remote region of the Great Desert of Araby lies the Rub'al Khali desert, or the Empty Quarter, a desolate expanse where, legend has it, the spirits of the dead and horrible creatures from other planes of reality are concealed. Many of them cannot adopt Euclidean forms in our reality. The wind in the Nameless City is often mistaken for these types of elemental entities. Among the sudden howling sandstorms, one frequently hears unspeakable secrets whispered by these creatures, and what appears to be a whimsical push turns out to be a trap that leads you to a horrible death.

Spawn of Abhoth

A creature that appears to be an amputated fragment of something much larger or, at least, more complete, although of rudimentary intelligence. They are described in the following way:

"Things like bodiless legs or arms that flailed in the slime, or heads that rolled, or floundering bellies with fishes' fins; and all manner of things malformed and monstrous, that grew in size as they departed from the neighborhood of Abhoth. And those that swam not swiftly ashore when they fell into the pool from Abhoth, were devoured by mouths that gaped in the parent bulk."

Cultists

People of both genders devoted to the obscure rites that worship the Cthulhu Mythos and other Great Old Ones.

George Aberdeen

An adventurous archeologist who embarks on the search of a mysterious city mentioned in the popular legends of Araby. Only his extensive knowledge of mythology and archaeology will let him uncover the mysteries of a city buried in sand which, prior to the existence of men, was dedicated to the worship of the Great Old One Hastur, father of Ithaqua and sibling of Cthulhu.

Inhabitants of the Nameless City

Old race that ruled the part of the world we now know as Araby, back in time immemorial. They built large cities of vast and complex beauty. Their body is the amalgamation of many mythological creatures: dragons, satyrs and other nameless creatures, heirs of the lizard-men. Word has it they used unconventional alien technology that has been lost to time.

Made in the USA
Middletown, DE
26 May 2023

31080578R00071